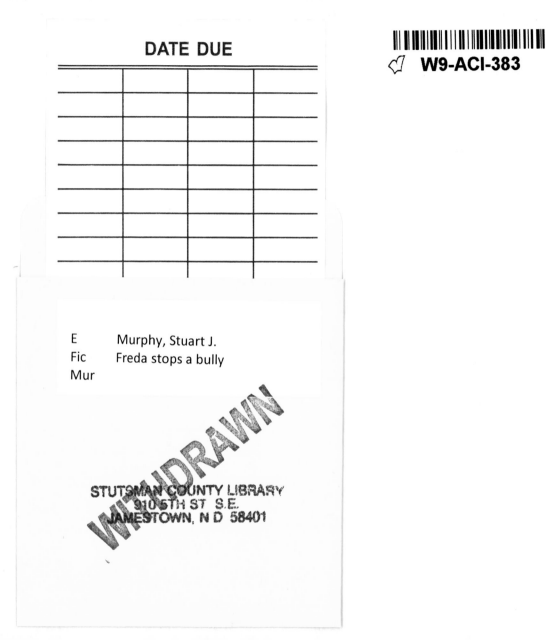

DATE DUE

W9-ACI-383

Freda loves her new pink shoes. But when she wears them, a boy at school teases her. What can Freda do to make the bully stop?

Percy

Art Avenue

Emma

Sunny Street

Wide Way

Fire Station

Freda

Center Circle

Welcome to
SEE-AND-**LEARN**
City

Ready
Set
Pre-K

Ajay

Stuart J. Murphy

Freda Stops a Bully

Emotional Skills: Dealing with Bullying

Stuart J. Murphy's

I See I Learn

Charlesbridge

Freda wore her favorite shoes to school.
They were bright pink.

A boy named Max said,
"Look at that girl with the funny shoes."
Then he yelled, "Funny Feet! Funny Feet!"

His friends laughed.
But Freda didn't think he was funny.

When Freda got home she put the shoes
in the back of her closet.

"What's wrong?" asked her mom.

"A boy at school made fun of my shoes," said Freda.

"I like your shoes," said her mom. "Maybe he just wants to impress his friends."

The next day Freda went to the park.
Percy and Emma were swinging on the swings.

Max was there, too.
"Hi, Funny Feet!" he hollered.
"Where are your funny shoes?"

Freda marched over to her mom.

"That boy hurt my feelings," said Freda.

"You can try not to listen to him," said her mom.

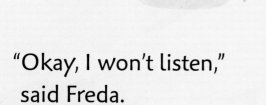

"Okay, I won't listen,"
said Freda.

Don't listen.

But Max didn't stop teasing Freda.
He kept calling out, "Funny Feet! Funny Feet!"

"Let's play somewhere else,"
said Percy.
They moved to another part
of the playground.

Walk away.

Max teased Freda every day at school.
"What are you going to do?" asked Emma.
"Maybe Miss Cathy can help," said Freda.

Freda and Emma went to see their teacher.
"I'll talk to Max," said Miss Cathy.
"He needs to know he is hurting your feelings."

Get help.

Before Miss Cathy could talk to Max,
Freda saw him in the playground.
"Here he comes," she said.
"Just tell him to stop," said Percy.

Say stop.

Max walked up to Freda.
"Hey, Funny Feet!" he said. "Hey, Funny—"
Freda turned to him. She was angry.

"Stop it!" she shouted.

"I was just trying to be funny," said Max.
"Well, I didn't think it was funny," said Freda.

The next day Freda wore her bright
pink shoes to school.
Max arrived wearing purple gym shoes
with stars on them.

He walked right up to Freda and said,
"Funny Feet! That's me!"
This time, *everyone* laughed.

What to do about a bully:

Don't listen.

Walk away.

Get help.

Say stop.

A Closer Look

1. How would **you** stop a bully?

2. Look at the pictures.
   What did Freda do to try to stop Max?

3. What did Percy and Emma do to help Freda?
   What would you do if you saw someone
   being bullied?

4. How would you feel if someone bullied you?
   How would others feel if you bullied them?

5. Draw a picture showing how Freda felt
   after she told Max to stop.

A Note About Visual Learning and Young Children

Visual Learning describes how we gather and process information from illustrations, diagrams, graphs, symbols, photographs, icons, and other visual models. Long before children can read—or even speak many words—they are able to assimilate visual information with ease. By the time they reach pre-kindergarten age (3–5), they are accomplished visual learners.

I SEE I LEARN™ books build on this natural talent, using inset pictures, diagrams, and highlighted words to help reinforce lessons conveyed through simple stories. The series covers social, emotional, health and safety, and cognitive skills.

Freda Stops a Bully addresses the emotional skill of dealing with bullies. Bullying is a serious issue, whether a child is being bullied, doing the bullying, or witnessing bullying as a bystander. Understanding what motivates the behavior can provide insights toward its resolution.

Let's all work together to stop bullying!

Photo © ArsAgassiz.com

Stuart J. Murphy is a Visual Learning specialist and the author of the award-winning MathStart series. He has also served as an author and consultant on a number of major educational programs. Stuart is a graduate of Rhode Island School of Design. He and his wife, Nancy, live in Boston, Massachusetts, near their children and three grandchildren, Jack, Madeleine, and Camille.

Text copyright © 2012 by Stuart J. Murphy
Illustrations copyright © 2012 by Tim Jones Illustration
All rights reserved, including the right of reproduction in whole or in part in any form. Charlesbridge and colophon are registered trademarks of Charlesbridge Publishing, Inc. Stuart J. Murphy's I See I Learn® and the Eyeglass Logo™ are trademarks of Stuart J. Murphy.

Published by Charlesbridge
85 Main Street
Watertown, MA 02472
(617) 926-0329
www.charlesbridge.com

Color separations by KHL Chroma Graphics, Singapore
Printed and bound February 2012 by Imago in Singapore

Library of Congress Cataloging-in-Publication Data
Murphy, Stuart J., 1942–
    Freda stops a bully / Stuart J. Murphy.
        p. cm. — (An I see I learn book. Emotional skills/Dealing with bullying)
    Summary: Max makes fun of Freda's shoes, but Freda soon learns how to cope with his bullying.
        ISBN 978-1-58089-466-1 (reinforced for library use)
        ISBN 978-1-58089-467-8 (softcover)
[1. Bullies—Fiction. 2. Schools—Fiction. 3. Life skills—Fiction. 4. Cats—Fiction. 5. Animals—Fiction.] I. Title. II. Series.
PZ7.M9563Ft 2012
813.54—dc23   2011026070

Printed in Singapore
(hc) 10 9 8 7 6 5 4 3 2 1
(sc) 10 9 8 7 6 5 4 3 2 1

Stuart J. Murphy's

I See I Learn®

teaches important skills for school readiness and daily life:

- **Social Skills**
- **Emotional Skills**
- **Health and Safety Skills**
- **Cognitive Skills**

Each book includes **A Closer Look:** two pages of activities and questions for further exploration.

Stuart J. Murphy is a Visual Learning specialist and the acclaimed author of the award-winning MathStart series.

www.iseeilearn.com

Charlesbridge
85 Main Street
Watertown, MA 02472
(617) 926-0329
www.charlesbridge.com